D0466269

First published in the United States 1999 by Dial Books for Young Readers
A member of Penguin Putnam Inc.
375 Hudson Street
New York, New York 10014
Published in Great Britain 1998 by
Bloomsbury Publishing Plc. as *The Photo*
Copyright © 1998 by Neal Layton
All rights reserved
Typography by Debora Smith
Printed in Belgium
First Edition
1 3 5 7 9 10 8 6 4 2

Library of Congress Cataloging in Publication Data
Layton, Neal.
Smile if you're human/story and pictures by Neal Layton.—1st ed.
p. cm.
Summary: An alien child's quest to take a photograph of a "mysterious creature known as a human"
has an unexpected result when a search through an Earth zoo brings an encounter with a gorilla.
ISBN 0-8037-2381-4
[1. Extraterrestrial beings—Fiction. 2. Zoos—Fiction. 3. Gorillas—Fiction.] I. Title.
PZ7.L44785Sm 1999
[E]-dc21 98-11482 CIP AC

SMILE
IF
YOU'RE
HUMAN

story and pictures by **Neal Layton**

Dial Books for Young Readers 🗼 New York

MAY 1999
SALINAS PUBLIC LIBRARY
— 1 2 3 4 5 6 7 8 9 10 11 12 13 14 15 16 17 18 19 20 21 22 23 24 25 26 27 28 29 30 31

Here we are landing at a place
I've wanted to visit my whole life.
It's a planet called "Earth."

On Planet Earth there are many animals.

I've brought my camera and hope
to take a picture of a most unusual
creature known as a "human."

We thought we saw one hopping around
in a green circular thing. "Is that a human?"
I asked my mom.

Mom looked at her book. "This jumpy fellow is a kangaroo. Humans like to walk."

As we spotted another animal,
I got my camera ready. "Look, Dad!
Humans are covered with stripes!"

"Hmm," said Dad, "I don't think so.
They don't have tails and they
mostly stand on two feet."

I raced up ahead.

ALIENS'
GUIDE
TO
EARTH

"What about these? They walk on two feet, and they seem very smart. They must be humans."

"They are smart," said Dad,
"but they're penguins.

Humans don't have wings or webbed feet."

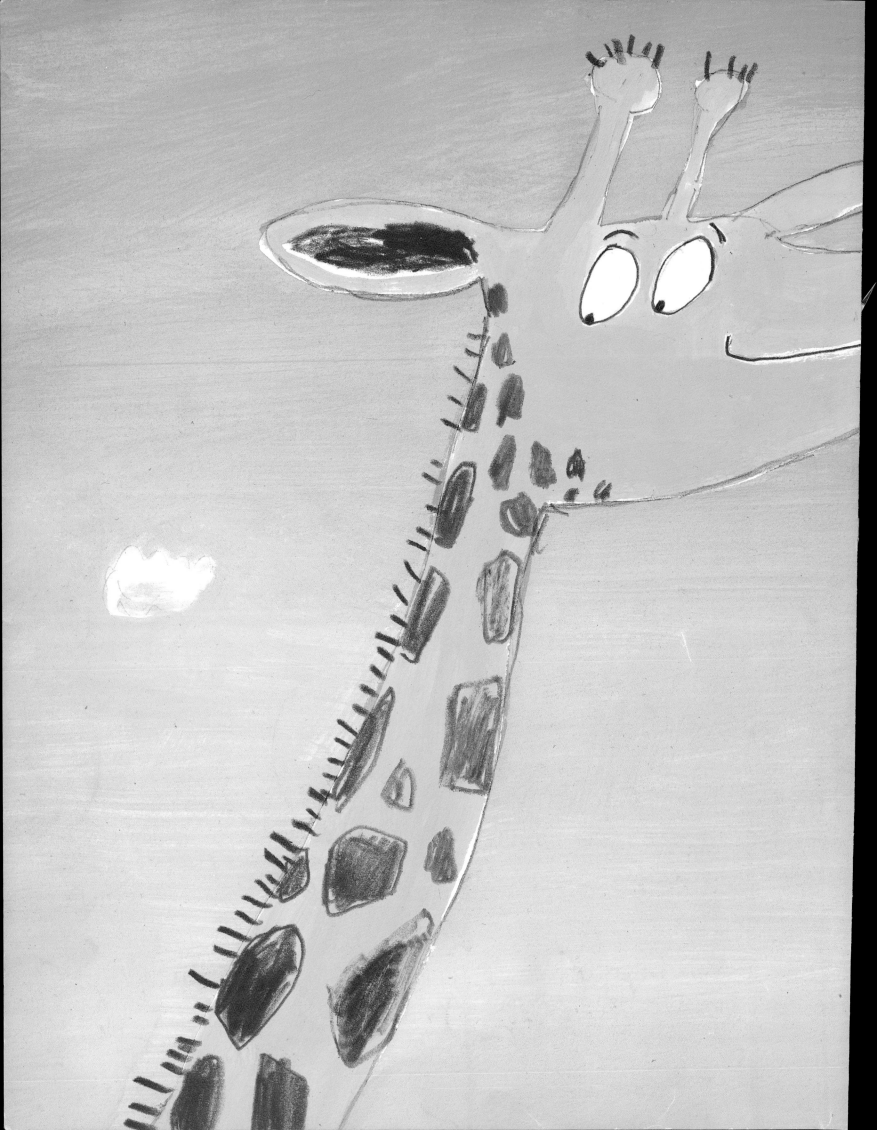

Just then I looked way, way up and
was sure I'd discovered a human.
"Wow, they're really tall!"

"Some humans are tall," Mom explained,
"but not **that** tall. This is a giraffe."

We had looked around
nearly the whole planet.

In the last house, we saw a
mysterious creature peeking out.

We got closer and I could see that it was . . . the most stupendous animal ever!

"Is it? IS IT?

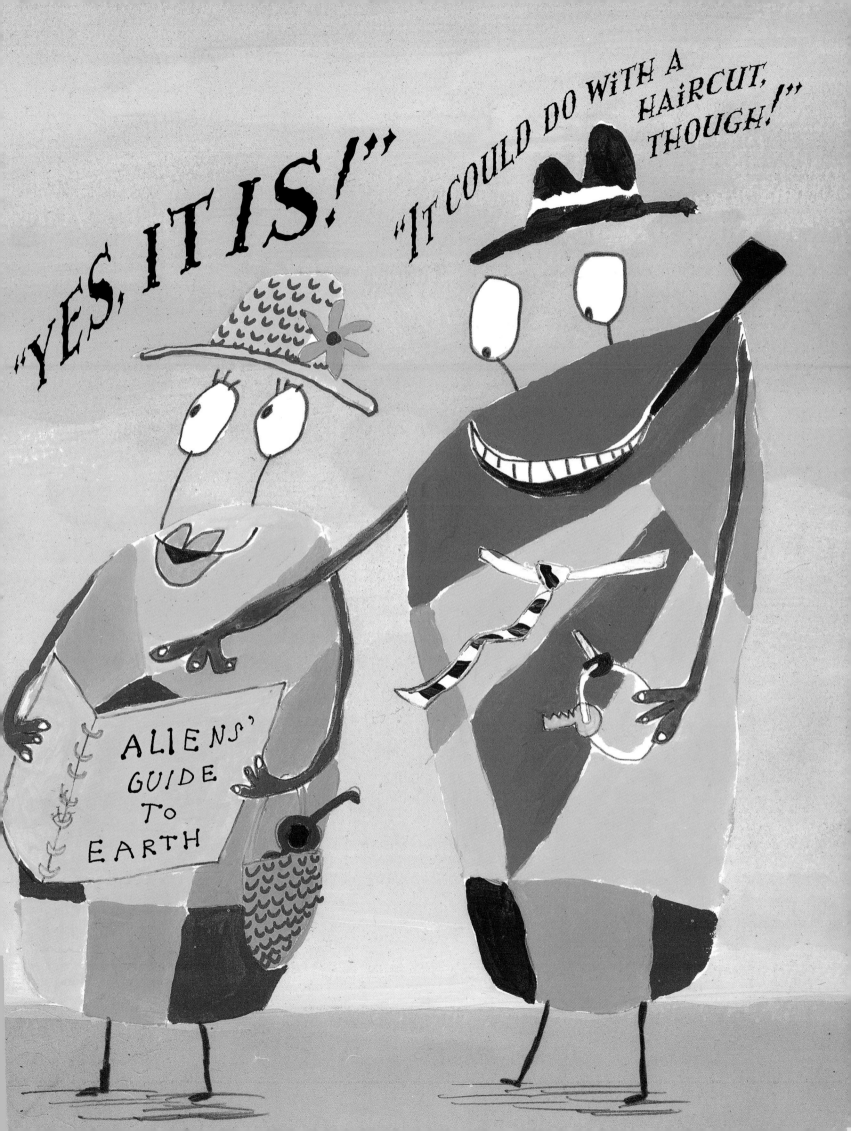

I steadied my camera,
took careful aim, and

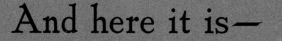

And here it is—

They don't have tails, or wings, or webbed feet; they're not great hoppers, or all **that** tall. But one thing for sure about humans— *they have the greatest smiles!*

APR
Rec
John Steinbeck
Library